Chapter 1

The legend.

In a gigantic, grassy forest called 'The Clawed Forest" lived two tribes of cats. One was the Sky tribe and the other was the Earth tribe. The Sky tribe live inside a huge, hollow willow tree trunk on the northern side of the forest, while the Earth tribe lives in an even bigger cave in the south. The two tribes lived together in companionship and harmony, but that would all change.

This story is about the legend of Shadow and Moonpaw, and how the feud between the Sky tribe and the Earth tribe started.

Many years ago, there was a young, pearly white furred, beautiful purple eyed Sky cat named Moonpaw. A gray cat with sky blue eyes called Shadow, (Also a Sky cat.) fell in love with the white beauty and Moonpaw loved him too.

Ash, a siamese Earth cat with lime eyes had feelings for Moonpaw and grew jealous of their love. He wanted Moonpaw all to himself, so one day, early one summer morning while the two cats were watching the sunset on the cliff of a waterfall on the eastern side of the forest, Ash attacked Shadow and pushed him off the cliff. Shadow died instantly. Hurt by the death of her loved one, she began to fight Ash. It was an endless battle, but eventually she won the fight.

When she told her tribe what had happened, they were furious. It started a huge war between the Sky and Earth tribe. The war finally ended with lots of scars and wounds. Since then, they never even looked at eachother.

And that's how the feud between the Sky tribe and the Earth tribe began.

Chapter 2

Grayswirl and Shiba.

Years later, the Sky tribe has a new leader by the name of Megaclaw, a giant, black smoke main coon with emerald green eyes. He may be rough and intimating at times, but he is a big hearted cat who loves his mate and kittens. He is fair to his troupers and always tries to do his best.

His mate, Hazel is a good hearted, brown tabby cat with rather bright orange eyes. Compassionate and caring, this gentle cat is a very protective of her kittens. But also wise and loving.

Together, they have four kittens. The oldest Acorn, Flower, Kibu and the youngest Grayswirl.

Being the oldest, Acorn (A ginger kitten with dark green eyes.) likes to believe that he is the wisest out of his siblings and likes to boss them around, a quality which annoy them.

Flower looks just like her dear mother,(Except for her father's eyes.) and tries to act like her too.

Kibu the third youngest on the other hand, is the spitting image of his father. (But with his mother's eyes.) He is quite a fierce and daring kitten, who loves to play with his siblings.

Grayswirl, as the smallest of her family she is very curious. But also adventures, fun loving and energetic. She is a gray cat with black swirls across her body. She has sky blue eyes that glow wherever she goes.

It was a warm, summer's day. Hazel was laying in the left had corner inside the tree trunk with her kittens beside her, licking them clean one by one.

"Can you tell us the story of Shadow and Moonpaw mother?" Grayswirl asked sweetly as it was her turn to be cleaned. (The kittens could never get enough of their mother's stories.)

"Grayswirl dear, I have already told you this story before." Hazel replied in her soft and gentle voice.

"Please mother!" The kittens begged.

Hazel sighed in defeat and began to tell the story, "A long time ago, before the Earth tribe and the Sky tribe . . ." but Megaclaw interrupted her as he walked towards them.

"Hazel, will you stop filling their heads with silly stories?" He said, smiling.

"They're not just stories Megaclaw, they're stories of the past." Hazel protested. "The kittens should know about these things."

Megaclaw shook his head in disagreement. "Listening to stories won't feed us." He exclaimed as he turned to the rest of the troupe.

He cleared his throat and announced to the others, "It's time for the hunt. Last night on my patrol I found a rat's burrow outside our territory. I would like two cats on the left side of the burrow and two cats on the right. I will be in front to make sure they don't get away. Let's move!" With that being said, him and the other males went out to hunt.

Acorn asked his mother if he and his siblings could play in the lake. His mother looked at him unsure. "I don't know, you kittens really shouldn't be out on your own."

The kittens begged until their mother gave in and said "Alright alright, you may go. But don't swim too deep, don't go into Earth troop's territory and be back before dark." She told them.

The kittens said their goodbyes and ran out of the tree and headed east towards the lake. They giggled as they splashed each other around, having the time of their lives.

Grayswirl's curiosity took control of her and while her siblings were too busy playing, she sneaked away. She desperately wanted to see the Earth troop's territory, so she ran off and soon enough she was standing in front of the cave which was five times bigger than the tree trunk. Suddenly, she heard footsteps coming out the cave. Quick as lighting, she hid in a nearby bush and hardly moved a muscle as the footsteps came closer and closer. All of a sudden, something tripped over Grayswirl.

It was a kitten, a calico kitten. It stared at Grayswirl with her elegant dark blue eyes, looking puzzled. Grayswirl was about to dash away before the kitten cried, Wait! Do you want to play with me?"

Grayswirl was very surprised by this kittens words. Her mother and father raised her to believe all Earth cats are evil, but the kittens sweet smile made Grayswirl think that maybe Earth cats aren't so bad after all. The grassy eyed calico kitten introduced herself as Shiba. The two of them played with each other and quickly became good friends. Unfortunately, it was almost dark by now and Grayswirl's father would be sure to scold her. They agreed to meet each other near the lake when the moon was in the center.

When the time came to meet her new friend by the lake, she managed to tiptoe out of the tree trunk and sprinted towards the lake where Shiba was waiting for her. They chased eachother around in the water, laughing like two hyenas. They stopped laughing instantly when they saw Megaclaw, (Grayswirl's father.) standing beside a bush, staring at the two kittens with eyes like fire.

"GRAYSWIRL, WHAT ARE YOU DOING?!" He shouted loudly, clearly livid. He stomped towards them and growled at Shiba, who was completely terrified. She began to shake uncontrollably with fear as this horrifying cat yelled, "DON'T YOU EVER COME NEAR MY KITTEN AGAIN! NOW LEAVE BEFORE I MAKE YOU!"

He raised his claws, threatening to swipe at her. Of course he wasn't going to as Megaclaw knew better than to hurt a kitten, even if it's from the Earth tribe. But he wanted to scare Shiba off. Poor Shiba ran home full of fear. Megaclaw picked his kitten up and walked back to the willow tree.

Chapter 3

Two friends reunited.

Ever since Grayswirl's father caught her playing with an Earth kitten, he made sure that she never stepped a claw out of the tree trunk ever again. No matter how much Grayswirl begged, her father refused to let her out. She was only allowed to go outside to have water when her mother takes her and her older siblings to the lake to have a drink.

After a very frightening scene with Megaclaw, (Grayswirl's father.) Shiba and Grayswirl stopped seeing each other. Over time, they forgot about one another and moved on with their lives.

It was only until Grayswirl was a fully grown cat that Megaclaw finally let his kitten go outside on her own. And that's when the two friends met again.

It was a cold, wintery evening and the Sky tribe was eating fish they had caught from the lake. Grayswirl was eating beside her mother, father and four older siblings. After her meal, Grayswirl felt thirsty so she left the tree trunk and walked over to the lake. She knelt down to take a sip when she saw a grassy green eyed calico cat coming down the path.

As soon as it saw Grayswirl, she extracted her claws and growled at her. Grayswirl could tell it was an Earth because she had never met it before, or so she thought.

"Why does she look so familiar?" Grayswirl thought. Then, it clicked. This is her old friend, Shiba.

"Shiba, is that you?" She asked, wide eyed with suprise.

The calico cat glanced at Grayswirl, utterly confused.

"How do you know my name?" She asked. "Who are you?"

"It's me, Grayswirl. We played together when we were kittens, remember?" Grayswirl explained to the puzzled grassy eyed calico. The calico thought for a few moments, then her eyes widened and her jaw dropped.

"Grayswirl?!" She said, excited to see her old friend. "Wow, you've grown!"

The two friends talked until it was time for Grayswirl to get back to the tree before her family got suspicious. Shiba suggested to Grayswirl if she would like to meet up again near the lake the next day, and Grayswirl said yes without hesitation. It made Grayswirl joyful to have a friend besides the other cats in the tribe.

That night, just before the moon was at it's highest, Grayswirl carefully creeped out of the tree trunk to meet her friend near the lake. Together, they sat on a curvy tree branch and talked on and on until the sun began to rise. They began to meet near the river in secret night after night for about four weeks.

On one of these particular nights, Shiba was sitting on the tree branch, waiting for her friend to arrive. After a while, Grayswirl still hadn't arrived. Soon, Shiba got tired of waiting and walked north towards the Sky tribe's Willow tree. She looked at it suprise. She never knew that willow trees can be that big. She stared at it for ten seconds before she stealthily sneaked inside. She looked around for Moonpaw, who was sleeping next to her older brothers and sister (Acorn, Flower and Kibu.) in a corner.

Silent as a mouse, she creaped up to Grayswirl and whispered in her ear, "Grayswirl, wake up."

Grayswirl sleepily opened her eyes. When she noticed that Shiba was standing right in front of her, she muttered anxiously, "Shiba, what are doing in here?! Someone'll see you!"

"Then let's go to the lake sleepyhead." Shiba whispered.

They quietly slipped away from the willow tree and headed to the lake. They sat on a tree branch and watched the sunset.

"Shiba, do you ever think about what it would be like if there wasn't a feud between our tribes?" Grayswirl asked her friend.

"Not much. I suppose the feud between the Earth tribe and the Sky tribe has been going on for so long, everyone's used to it." Shiba answered.

Grayswirl sighed and said, "It's not right. Just because of something from the past, doesn't mean we can't live in harmony in companionship like we did years ago before the war. Someone has to stop it or else it will get worse."

Shiba smiled at her friend, impressed by her desire to stop the feud between the Sky tribe and the Earth tribe. "Wise words, my friend. I agree, the feud has been going on for too long. If you ever need help with stopping the feud, I'll be here for you." She said, putting her paw on Grayswirl's.

Grayswirl thanked Shiba for being a loyal friend. They continued to talk until well into the morning. Before the two friends knew it, the afternoon came. They were usually very careful to arrive home before by early morning, but today they got so busy talking that they forgot the time.

Back in the willow tree while the other cats were asleep, Megaclaw woke up to realise that his youngest daughter wasn't sleeping beside her brothers and sister. He began to get worried as any father would. He stretched out his legs, stood up and started to look for Grayswirl.

This caused his mate, Hazel to wake up and saw how worried he was so she quietly asked, yawning, "What's wrong, dear?"

"Grayswirl isn't inside the tree." He whispered in response, getting more and more worried. "I'm going to go into the forest to look for her. What if she got hurt?!"

"Calm down, I'm sure she's fine. After all, she's a full grown cat now. She probably went to the lake to have a drink. She'll be back soon." Hazel murmured, reassuring her mate.

"I'll go to the lake, just to see if she's alright. I'll be back." With those words, careful not to wake anyone up stepped out of the tree of sleeping cats and walked to the lake. As he walked up to the lake, he heard a voice. He pricked his ears up and listened carefully. He realised that it was his daughter's voice, so he followed it to quite a curvy tree. He look looked up and saw Grayswirl sitting on a branch with an Earth cat and the moment he saw them, anger flared up inside him.

"GRAYSWIRL, WHAT ARE YOU DOING?!" He shouted. Grayswirl and Shiba almost fell off the tree branch with fright.

"Shiba, run!" Grayswirl cried with fear.

Megaclaw climed up the curvy tree to attack Shiba, but Shiba was too quick for him. She rushed away, leaping from one tree to another. Within seconds, she was out of sight. Grayswirl was full of relief that Shiba got away in time, her father (Megaclaw.) on the other hand was livid.

"HOW DARE YOU TALK TO THIS EARTH CAT! YOU KNOW EARTH CATS ARE EVIL!" Megaclaw roared at Grayswirl.

"I'm sorry father. I . . ." Grayswirl stammered, startled by her father's growl.

"I WILL NOT ACCEPT THIS BEHAVIOUR FROM MY OWN DAUGHTER! I AM YOUR LEADER, AND YOU WILL DO AS I SAY, UNDERSTAND?!"

Seeing her father's mood, Grayswirl timidly nodded her head and muttered, "Yes father."

They climbed down the curvy tree and walked back to the huge willow tree in complete silence. It actually made Grayswirl slightly nervous.

Chapter 4

War.

The next morning, Megaclaw's temper still hadn't cooled down because he woke up all the sleeping cats with his echoing voice saying, "Wake up and listen, this is very important. I am declaring war on the Earth tribe! I think it's about time those evil cats learned their lesson! Now are you going to defend your tribe or lay here useless as slugs?"

Grayswirl's eyes widened when she heard this. She quickly stood up and cried, "Father, you can't do that! The Earth tribe did nothing to us!"

"Silence!" Megaclaw snapped at her. "You asked for it when you were talking with that Earth cat yesterday. The other cats gasped. You betrayed your tribe." He added, looking at his daughter in disappointment. "You will stay here where you are safe from those evil cats. Sky cats, let's go!"

The cats obeyed his command and walked out of the tree, leaving Grayswirl behind.

Grayswirl sat there, not knowing what to do. After staring at the wall for about thirty seconds, she realised that she can't just sit there doing nothing. The tribes were about to go into war and she had to stop it.

She dashed out of the willow tree headed straight for the middle of the forest, where she saw cats scratching and biting eachother until some blood was drawn. It was a horrible sight.

"STOP!" Grayswirl shouted, so loud that all the cats stopped fighting and turned to her. Grayswirl could make out the face of her angry father, who was about to scratch a ginger cat's face. He looked dreadful with a cut on his ear now bleeding and another slash on his left leg also bleeding.

"Grayswirl, what are you doing?" He grumbled.

"This fued has to end." Grayswirl proclaimed.
"It's been going on for too long." She walked
over to her father.

"Do you remember when you said Earth cats
are evil?" She asked him. "Well that isn't true.
And do you know how I know that? Because my
friend is an Earth cat. Just because an Earth
cat did an evil thing in the past, that doesn't
mean all the Earth cats will." She continued her
speech as she looked at the Earth cats, most of
them scratched badly.

"Even if they're from a different tribe, they're
cats like us. We're all the same father, just look
at them and you'll see it."

Megaclaw looked around at the Earth cats for a moment and understood what his daughter was saying. He rubbed his head on hers, showering his daughter love. He then looked at the crowd of scratched up cats and said, "What my daughter said is true. It's time we stop this feud, and live peacefully like we used to."

"I agree." Spoke the Sky tribe's leader, a white cat with large ginger spots and hazel eyes. He would've looked quite nice if he didn't have so many scratches on him. "There's no use in keeping this feud up. I say we start again."

Thanks to Grayswirl, from that day on Sky cats and Earth cats lived together in harmony.

Printed in Great Britain
by Amazon